CLOUD WARRIOR

ERIN FANNING

SADDLEBACK
EDUCATIONAL PUBLISHING

MONARCH JUNGLE

SADDLEBACK
EDUCATIONAL PUBLISHING
www.sdlback.com

Copyright ©2018 by Saddleback Educational Publishing
All rights reserved. No part of this book may be reproduced in any form or by any means, electronic or mechanical, including photocopying, recording, scanning, or by any information storage and retrieval system, without the written permission of the publisher. SADDLEBACK EDUCATIONAL PUBLISHING and any associated logos are trademarks and/or registered trademarks of Saddleback Educational Publishing.

ISBN-13: 978-1-68021-476-5
ISBN-10: 1-68021-476-4
eBook: 978-1-63078-830-8

Printed in Guangzhou, China
NOR/1117/CA21701345

22 21 20 19 18   1 2 3 4 5

MONARCH
JUNGLE

Chapter 1

Sun and Shadows

Ask me my favorite sport. I'd have to say kayaking. It's good exercise. And it's a mental workout too. There's something about facing the elements. It tests every part of you. Sunny weather is a bonus. But this is Saddle City. Chances of sun in the mountains are fifty-fifty.

It was just after sunrise. I rode with my dad. Two kayaks were in the back of his pickup. My best friend, Juan, was in his truck. He followed us to a fishing site. That's where he left his truck. Then we drove on to the launch site. From here, Juan and I would paddle back.

My dad helped us unload the kayaks. Then we slid them into the water and got in. Our 15-mile ride started now. We waved back at my dad and started paddling.

Juan and I had been here before. We knew Blackwater River well. It was broken up into sections. The upper part was mostly flat. The water was calm. Earlier I'd checked the forecast. So far it was in my favor.

A few minutes had gone by. I looked up at the sky. There were a few gray patches. Though I was no expert, I knew clouds. These led to rain. So much for the forecast.

The rest of the sky was blue. We'd be fine, I told myself. But one thought nagged at me. Clouds don't lie.

"Let's pick up the pace." I pointed up with my paddle. "See those clouds? We need to get ahead of them."

Juan was eating an energy bar. "Wait, don't tell me. They spoke to you." He laughed so hard, bits of food flew from his mouth.

"Keep your mouth shut, fool. Remember who you're talking to."

"So sorry, Cloud Warrior. But I say you're wrong. Those clouds look harmless." Juan laughed.

"Go ahead. Laugh. I'll enjoy seeing that smirk wiped off your face."

Juan jabbed his middle finger at me. "Whatever." He took off paddling.

I surged toward him. "What's with you?"

"What do you mean? I'm being my usual charming self. It's why the babes drool over me."

"Rabid dogs drool over you."

"I have my admirers." A zit on his nose shone in the sun.

"Have you looked in a mirror? We're not exactly sex symbols."

"Speak for yourself," Juan said.

I was. Most girls in my class towered over me. I wore glasses. My ears stuck out. And I was already losing my hair.

Our look was not high fashion. At school, we wore whatever was clean. On the water, we looked really sloppy. Wide-brimmed hats. Ragged shorts and T-shirts. Our life vests had some style. But we'd end up covered in mud anyway.

The kayaks didn't look so good either. Mine had bird poop on it. It was baked on by the sun. Juan's had oil splatters from working on his truck.

We weren't cool. But we were prepared. Our dry bags carried supplies. Rope. Flashlights. First-aid kit. Extra clothes. Water and snacks.

Juan's paddle sliced the water in rhythm with mine.

"It's getting hot," Juan said. He pushed up his sleeves.

Normally we wouldn't be sweating this soon. But the air was so dry. Another sign of a storm. "It won't last," I told Juan. "We just have to get ahead of the weather." I wasn't going to let anything ruin this trip.

Tangled

Juan and I paddled in silence. The water was calm. We leaned into the breeze.

Pine trees lined the shore. Hawks flew overhead. Fish jumped out of the water. It was a perfect day.

Just ahead was a dam. The river became a reservoir. It was called Cub Lake. Beyond that, the river picked up again. That's when the paddling really began.

Fast water made it a fun ride. And though still easy, some skill was needed. Mainly it was watching for obstacles. Rocks. Small logs. Tree limbs. The hardest part would be the waves. But even those were mild. All of it was a warm-up for later.

After a while, we paddled across Cub Lake. It was a great spot for fishing. Families camped here. It seemed odd that no one was around. There was only an eerie quiet. Was it some kind of omen? Maybe they knew something I didn't.

I hadn't checked the dam's release schedule. Now I wished I had. The water level could rise with no warning. But it was too late to worry. Today was a holiday. No one was working. I wasn't even sure I could get a phone signal.

Suddenly there was a noise. It broke through the quiet. I couldn't quite make it out. But it wasn't from nature. "Hear that?"

Juan nodded. We slowed our paddling.

"Over there," I said.

There were three guys and a girl. The guys were yelling. The girl was sitting with her knees drawn up. Her arms were wrapped around her legs.

Juan froze. "Maria?"

I couldn't tell. The girl's hair blew across her face. It was a tangled mess. But I wasn't taking chances. I started paddling.

The wind had picked up. A wave sloshed over the bow of my kayak. I looked at the girl again. She moved her hair from her face. It *was* Maria.

The voices got louder. I continued to watch. One guy was doing most of the talking. He paced back and forth. His movements were frantic. Then I noticed his muscles. They were huge. If a fight broke out, the two smaller guys would lose.

Now their faces were visible. I knew them. One was Tyler. He was Maria's boyfriend. The other was Chris. He used to be my friend. Somewhere along the line, he turned into a loser. If he wasn't skipping school, he was busy scoring weed. This kid did not fit in with Maria and Tyler. They were popular. Chris was not cool at all.

The big guy looked older. At first I didn't recognize him. Then I remembered. He worked at Burger Bar. I hadn't been there in a while. But at that time, he had short hair. Now it was long and he had a beard. I wondered if he'd been fired.

Tyler stood next to Maria. Chris walked over to the edge of the woods. He stood in front of a campfire. Behind him was a tent.

"Hold on, Raul," Juan yelled.

Maria's head whipped around. Juan's voice must have carried to shore. I noticed the shadows under Maria's eyes. Her skin wasn't its normal brown. It looked gray.

Mr. Muscles had also heard Juan. Now he ran in our direction. Not sure what to do, I waved. I must have looked like a dork sitting there bobbing up and down.

"Don't call attention to us," Juan said. His kayak bumped into mine. "Let's keep going. We can pretend we don't see them."

"Something weird is going on. We can't leave Maria," I said.

"Yeah, well, she chose her friends a long time ago."

"That's harsh."

Maria had dropped us for the cool kids. Juan had never forgiven her. I could forgive anything when it came to Maria.

Right now I wanted to fly across the water—with or without a kayak. I started paddling with long forward strokes.

"Easy, lover boy," Juan said. "You don't want to get too close. We can't help Maria if those guys kill us."

I slowed down. "You're right. We'll stay back."

"And be cool."

"That's not easy for you and me."

Juan laughed. "Not easy for you."

Danger

We were now close to shore. "Hi, Maria," I called out. "Hey, Tyler."

Tyler stood over Maria. A wide, creepy smile stretched across his face. It was straight out of a horror movie. Maria didn't move or speak. Chris poked at the fire with a stick.

"How's it going, Chris?" Juan asked.

"Great. Nice day, isn't it?"

Tyler stepped forward. "Hey, Cloud Warrior." Then he nodded at Juan. "How's it going, Stinky Feet?"

Juan flinched. I rolled my eyes. These names were from fourth grade. I often wondered if anyone knew our real names.

My nickname came from a school assignment. It was

on family heritage. We had to give a report on our ancestors. Mine are from Peru. They lived during the time of the Incas. The Chachapoya. It means "Cloud people." They had been fighters, called "Cloud warriors." Kids started calling me that. But I didn't mind back then. I loved clouds. I still do.

Juan got his nickname that same year. He had bad foot odor. It was so rank that kids in his PE class got sick. One boy even puked. Juan's hygiene got a lot better. But no one would let him forget.

Maria's eyes were wide. She blinked a few times. It was an attempt to tell me something. But what? Mr. Muscles whispered in her ear. Then he looked over at us. "Nice day for paddling," he said. He squeezed Maria's shoulder. She held up a limp hand. Her fingers fluttered in a sort of wave.

"I remember you from the burger place. You're …"

"Steve," he said.

"Right. What are you guys doing out here? Fishing?"

"Oh my God," Juan said in a low voice. "Is that the best you could come up with? Do you see any gear?"

"Yeah, you could say that," Steve said. "We're fishing. Right, Tyler?"

"Um, sure." Tyler shifted his weight from one foot to the other. He forced the creepy smile again.

Maria squirmed under Steve's grip. He clamped down even harder. "Say hello to your friends, Mary."

When Maria joined the popular crowd, she gave up her Spanish name.

"Hi, Raul," she said.

"Want to go fishing with us?" Steve asked. "The more the merrier." He looked at Tyler and smiled. "Right?"

Tyler wobbled. He looked like he might fall over.

Chris stood against a tree. He was eating something. Then he coughed and waved his hands. I couldn't tell if he was choking or warning me.

Steve went over to Chris. "Let me help you," Steve said. He reached out and grabbed one of Chris's arms. The motion pulled Steve's T-shirt up. Something metallic glinted in the sun. It could have been a gun. Before I could tell, the shirt fell back into place.

"Sounds good," I said. "But I think we'll have to pass. Right, Juan?"

I looked around. Juan was already paddling toward the dam.

"See you later," I said.

"Hold on," Steve shouted.

I glanced over my shoulder. Chris held up a beer in a toasting gesture. Tyler wrapped an arm around Maria. She moved to get away from him.

"*Ayudame*," she mouthed. It was Spanish for *help me*.

I took out my cell phone. No signal. When I glanced over, I saw Steve. He walked quickly along the shoreline. Juan and I would get around the dam before he reached it. Steve had a long way to go. I took off paddling.

Disturbed

Looking back at the shore, I saw Maria. She was in the lake. Water skimmed the bottom of her shorts. It looked like she might swim out to me. I wouldn't mind. But my kayak had one seat. So, like a moron, I turned around and went back.

I couldn't figure it out. Why didn't she and Tyler just leave? The parking lot wasn't that far.

"Come on!" Juan yelled. He was near the dam. His kayak bobbed up and down. "Don't be stupid!"

He was right. When it came to Maria, my mind was mush. As I turned around, I nodded at her. She had to know I'd go for help.

Just then a branch snapped. Steve came out from the trees. "Need help?"

"No thanks. I'm good." I put as much power behind my paddle as I could. The kayak flew through the water.

When I reached the dam, I saw Juan. He was dragging his kayak through the weeds. Then he disappeared down a path.

I jumped out of my kayak. It nearly flipped in the process. The muddy bottom of the river sucked at my shoes. And then I saw Steve. He stood high on a ridge. I wasn't worried. It would take him forever to reach the dam. Juan and I would be long gone.

Steve lit a cigarette. He glared at me and tossed the match. It landed in the brush. Great. All we needed was a fire. I smiled and gave him a wave. There was no need to provoke the guy.

He gave me a thumbs-down. What he meant wasn't clear. But it wasn't a good sign. The guy seemed a little off. Who knew what he had in mind? I wasn't going to wait to find out.

I pulled my kayak to the dam. Juan was waiting. We looked up at the structure. It stood about four feet above us. Water spilled over the top of a wooden gate.

The wind had picked up. I got my jacket out of the dry pack and put it on.

"That gate looks old," Juan said.

I scanned the slats of the gate. They ran side to side,

sitting in a track. Pins on each side held them in place. The water was released by pulling out the pins.

The gate was locked. But that wouldn't matter if the boards broke. Right now, water leaked between the slats. We'd have a wild ride if it burst through. Our kayaks weren't made for whitewater.

"Think we'll be okay?" Juan asked.

"What else could go wrong?"

Juan wasn't smiling. Had I just jinxed us? We dragged our kayaks back to the water.

Chapter 5

Stuck

We were now mid-river. The water had a light current. There were a few small waves. I remembered there being a stretch of brush and overhanging trees. But other than that, it was an easy ride.

Juan got into his kayak. He shoved off using the tip of his paddle. The water pulled him around a bend and out of sight.

As I pushed off, I smelled cigarette smoke. Steve was nearby. After a few minutes, I saw Juan ahead. He had gotten out of his kayak. It was wedged between a boulder and the shore. He held his cell phone.

"Any luck?" I called.

"No signal." He shoved the phone into his pocket. "Do you want to land and find a spot?"

"We need to stay ahead of Steve. Let's go a little farther. Then we can stop and hike out of here."

"Sounds good."

He got back into his kayak and pushed off. I followed him.

"Hey," Juan said. "Was that a gun Steve had? Or did I imagine it?"

"It looked like a gun to me."

"What are Maria and Tyler doing with him?"

"No idea," I said. "But it's not Tyler I care about."

"I know. We were never buddies with him. But face it, Raul. We don't know Maria anymore."

Juan was right about Tyler. But Maria seemed the same to me.

The river had been clear until this point. Now we'd come up on a fallen tree. We managed to squeeze around it. But the next obstacle wouldn't be so easy. A beaver dam ran the width of the river. It was a line of logs and small, sharp branches.

We had three options. Get out and drag our kayaks over it. That was the last resort. Get to the bank and carry our kayaks around. In this case, the bank was too steep and swampy. The third option was to paddle over it. The drop over the dam was only about a foot. So we opted for that.

Hitting the dam at high speed, we got part way up.

Then we jerked our way to the top and flew down. Our kayaks took a beating. But we didn't tip over.

The beaver dam made me think of Chris. Beaver had been his nickname. It was due to having buckteeth. Original.

At the time, Chris laughed it off. Finally he got braces. But he changed. He dropped us for the stoners. Before, he'd hung out with Maria, Juan, and me.

The river now widened. The current slowed. I could no longer see the bottom. Juan and I floated along. A light wind was at our backs. It felt good.

"What happened to Chris?" I asked.

"That was a long time ago," Juan said. "Maybe it had to do with his mom. She took off and left him. Remember? Then Chris and his dad moved out of our neighborhood. They lived in those crappy apartments."

"I don't remember any of that."

Chris had changed about the same time Maria dropped us. I hadn't noticed. I'd been too wrapped up in my own problems.

"Did his mom ever come back?" I asked.

"I don't know. Does it matter? He'll never be the same. Even Maria is so different. Think about it. She's out in the woods drinking and smoking."

"We don't know she's part of that."

"Maybe Tyler and Maria are out here buying weed."

"Doubt it." I steered around a rock. "But I know one thing. Maria needs our help."

"I know. You want to be her hero. And it's the right thing to do. I guess."

"You know it is."

Chapter 6

Daze

Saddle City is a small town. New people stand out. It's the same with high school. New kids get noticed. They fit in. Or they don't.

When Maria started school, I was curious. Of course I liked her looks. She was so pretty. But it was more than that. No one spoke to her. She hung out alone.

I didn't go up to her either. Why would she talk to me? So I asked around. Maria's family had moved here from Mexico. She didn't speak much English.

One day I said hi in Spanish. It was the first time I'd seen her smile. Juan and I asked her to join us. From then on we were friends. We had so much fun. We kayaked and fished and went biking.

Sometimes a girl comes between guys. This wasn't

like that. Mainly it gave Juan a break. Get me talking, and I can't stop. Juan would rather sleep than listen. Now he didn't have to. Maria could do it. And she did.

She liked the whole cloud thing. We'd lie on our backs and stare at the sky. "Read the clouds," she'd say. It made me feel good. For the first time, I was proud to be a geek.

I'd talk about the Cloud warriors as Juan rolled his eyes. By now he had it memorized. They were a hill tribe from Peru. The forests were their home. Their kingdom stretched across the mountains. It seemed to touch the clouds. The people were fierce fighters. And they had great respect for their ancestors.

Maria didn't laugh at my nickname. "Cloud Warrior," she'd said. "It suits you."

I thought the three of us would always be friends. Then Juan pointed something out. Maria was changing. "Don't you see it?" he'd asked. Maria had a new look. She wore more makeup. And she was flirting with guys. That got my attention. In my mind, we were more than friends.

Then everything changed. Maria now went by Mary. Slowly she dropped Spanish and her accent. Juan and I were next.

I didn't think she meant to hurt us. It's what she had

to do to be popular. I got that. But Juan felt let down. Maybe it was stupid of me. But I couldn't let go. I wanted Maria back. She was worth waiting for.

♔

Gray clouds filled the sky. Rain pinged our kayaks. The wind had changed direction. It was no longer at our backs. Paddling was much harder.

"Here comes the storm," Juan said. He cinched the drawstring on his hat.

Maria's silent "help me" came to mind. I imagined her trapped inside the tent. Steve held the gun on her. Tyler was helpless to do much. Chris was too stoned to care. I paddled faster.

Now the sky was dark. The river narrowed, and the shore rose above us. A crackling sound rang out. It was followed by a loud boom.

"Thunder," Juan said. "Now we're in trouble."

"Maybe the lightning will hold off."

"Not with our luck."

"Look for a place to stop," I called. "We can wait for the storm to pass."

Juan pointed toward shore. "What about up there? That ledge."

I nodded.

"We can try our phones," Juan said.

A current shoved us along. We were paddling into a strong headwind. There was no chance to get to shore.

The river was not supposed to be wild. Water rose up in high waves and swamped my kayak. I was soaked.

There were no signs of hypothermia yet. I was just cold. If my feet and hands went numb, I'd be in trouble. I wondered how Juan was doing.

Chapter 7

Spiral

Trees swayed. Branches snapped and fell. I was afraid of being hit. I'd drown if I got knocked out. Fear welled up inside. I tried to focus. It helped to keep my eyes on Juan.

As I trailed behind him, I saw waves rise. They towered above his kayak. The bow started to go through the water. But then it rose up. Coming down, his kayak hit a rock.

Juan rolled to one side. He tried to get level. But it was too late. Water flooded his kayak. It tipped and he fell into the river. His life vest inflated. I watched as he floated downstream.

Just then a log raced by. "Look out!" I shouted. But Juan had vanished.

A small wave hit me from the side. My kayak tilted.

It half filled up with water. I quickly got level. But a new danger waited.

It was a whirlpool. I knew to stay out of the center. It can suck you under. Instead, I stayed on the outer edge. Its energy pulled me around until I shot downstream. I stopped a few feet from the bank.

My nerves were on edge. I decided to land. Normally I'd find a calm section. But I might not get that chance. It had to be now while I was able.

I grabbed my bag and paddle. Slowly I got out of the kayak. The water was hip high. I stood between the river and the kayak. One wave would carry it away.

My luck ran out a long time ago. A wave hit the kayak. It slipped from my hands. Then the worst happened. The kayak got stuck between some boulders. I'd have to leave it.

Time was running out. Juan could be pinned by the log. Worse, he was drowning or already dead.

I waded toward shore. Water pulled at my legs. They felt like lead weights. Finally I was at the bank. It was close enough to touch. I tossed the paddle and bag onto shore. Then I reached out to grab land. The surface was slippery. My hands came back with clumps of mud.

Thinking fast, I grabbed a tree root. Slowly I pulled myself from the water. Prickly weeds stung my hands and knees. As I stood up, I felt dizzy. My whole body shivered. I put on the extra clothes from my bag. Then it began to rain. Was this nature's way of joking?

A storm was one thing. But the raging water didn't make sense. There'd never been a strong current like this. The dam must have burst. Or the gate was opened. Wait! Steve had been near the dam. Maybe he did it.

Water washed over the shore. There was only one way out. I headed into a wooded area. The sudden darkness blinded me. I stumbled over roots and around trees. Branches scratched my hands and face.

A hill was ahead. I scrambled to the top. The river raged below. It wasn't a straight drop. But it was close.

This side of the hill was rocky. So I was able to sit and inch my way down. Near the bottom, I stood up. Right away, I slipped on some loose pebbles. My feet came out from under me. I fell and slid on sand. The river was coming closer.

Hold On

Small shrubs along the shore had stopped my fall. As I sat there, I saw an object. There was a log in the river. Debris gathered in its branches. Something was sticking out. It was a hand. All I could think was that an animal had torn some person apart.

My stomach clenched. Vomit rose up into my throat. I forced it down. That's when I saw fingers. They wiggled. "Juan?"

I crawled onto the log. Juan looked up at me. Water lapped at his face. Where was the rest of him? I looked over and saw his shoes. That was a relief. Still, I felt dread.

"Are you okay?" I asked.

Juan tried to speak. Instead, he gasped for air.

"Keep your head up," I said. "Try not to swallow water."

Now I saw what held Juan up. His vest was caught on a branch. It had kept him from drowning. I looked around for his kayak. There was no sign of it.

He tried to move. That's when his vest ripped. His chin sunk below the water. Soon his mouth would be covered too.

"Try to stay calm," I told him. "Breathe." Juan could pass out if he panicked.

Using my paddle for balance, I stepped across the log. The current nearly ripped it from my hand. I tripped and fell hard. But the pain didn't register. It took everything I had not to fall into the water.

I wrapped my limbs around the log. Then I dropped my paddle. It lay among the debris. I grabbed it and crawled forward. But then I fell again. I let out a groan. Then it came to me. I'd gone about this all wrong. A better plan was to work from the bank.

I scooted backward until my feet hit land. Sitting on the bank, I reached out with my paddle. Juan flinched as it hit his head. But he managed to grab onto it.

With my feet pressed against the log, I tugged. Juan's head popped up. Hand over hand, he pulled himself toward me.

His vest ripped on branches. Then his hands slid off the paddle. The current sucked him back. He lurched to his feet, up to his hips in water. Then he lunged for the paddle. Holding it, he struggled to shore while I tugged from my end. The current battled him every step.

Once on shore, he collapsed. We stared at each other. We were both too tired to speak. But there wasn't time to sit around. The sun would be going down in a few hours.

I looked at Juan in his wet clothes. His lips were blue. As he closed his eyes, I prodded him with my foot.

"Hey. No kicking," he mumbled.

"Are you okay? I mean, can you walk?"

"Why? Are you going to carry me if I can't?"

"That's the Juan I know. Always making jokes." I smiled. It was a good feeling. But it only lasted for a second.

Chill

I'll be fine," Juan said. "I'm just a little shaky." He stood and then sat back down.

I dumped out my bag. "Here, eat this." I tossed him an energy bar. "And then get changed." I pointed to a sweatshirt and pair of shorts.

"We're going for a little walk," I said. "Back to my kayak. If we can find it. Last I saw it, it was stuck."

I tucked a flashlight into my pocket. Juan put the clothes on. Then he grabbed a small knife.

It wasn't an easy hike. The way I'd come wasn't marked. But finally I saw the kayak. It moved a little in the rushing water. Most of it was covered. Soon the rapids would carry it away.

As Juan sat studying the river, I noticed he was shivering.

"I hit a rock. Then I was thrown from my kayak," he said. "I must have been hit by the log. Somehow I got tangled up in the branches. And the kayak kept going. My paddle, dry bag, everything is gone."

"But here you are. And looking so stylish in my clothes."

Juan looked down at the frayed sweatshirt. "I'd hate to see the rest of your wardrobe. No wonder Maria doesn't like you."

"You have a point." I laughed but not for long.

Water covered my kayak. Steve waited for us—possibly with a gun. And our phones were dead.

"Speaking of Maria," I said. "We have to go back."

"Yeah, you keep saying that. How close are we to my truck?"

"We'll have to get it later. Besides, Cub Lake is closer. From the campground, we can hike out to the main road. Maybe flag down a car and get help."

"That's a big maybe." Juan stared at the river again. "What do you think happened? Why did the river suddenly turn wild?"

"It must have been the dam. Maybe it burst. Or someone messed with it."

"How?" Juan asked.

"We'll check it out on the way back."

I twisted my paddle apart. I handed one end to Juan. "Here, take this. I'll use the other end."

"For what?"

"As a walking stick. Or a weapon. You know, like a bat."

"Sure. That'll work. 'Put the gun down, Steve. I've got a bat.' "

"It's better than nothing," I said.

Now came the part when Juan called me loco. But he didn't argue. Instead, he took the paddle. I repacked my gear and tied the bag around my waist. Then we headed for the dam.

As we hiked in silence, the sky burst open. Sheets of rain poured down. I felt the water run down my neck and back. Then lightning crackled, followed by the roar of thunder.

I trudged after Juan. Our feet sloshed inside our shoes. *Think. Think. Think*, I said to myself. Nothing came to mind, except a sense that I was freezing. The temperature felt 20 degrees cooler than it had earlier. And it would only get worse.

Rivers changed in an instant. Weather was that way too. I knew all that. Yet here we were caught in a storm. The rest of this trip was supposed to be easy. *Cloud Warrior. What a joke.*

Chapter 10

Confused

We climbed a hill to get a look at the dam. Water poured through the gate. Some boards were missing.

"It looks too neat," I said. "Wouldn't the water have busted the boards?"

"Let's get a closer look." Juan stepped forward.

"Hold on." I pulled him back by his arm. "Let's make sure no one's around."

"You really think we'll see anyone? Only fools would be out in this storm."

I shot Juan a dirty look. "Rub it in."

With any luck, he was right. Maria was at home and safe. But my gut said something else.

The sun was getting low in the sky. Soon the temperature would drop. We had to work fast. Juan and I inched across the top of the dam. Water swirled below. As I looked down, I teetered. Juan grabbed my arm to steady me.

"Easy there, Cloud Warrior. Do you have the flashlight?"

I pulled it out of my pocket. "Here."

He aimed the beam toward the gate. We could see the lock was missing. Someone had taken the boards out on purpose.

"Whoever did it had a key," Juan said.

"No. Look." I aimed the beam at the ground. There was the lock. It was broken.

Thunder rumbled in the sky. It was like the sound I'd heard minutes before the river turned wild.

"Steve does have a gun," I said.

"What are you saying?"

"Don't you see? He shot the lock off."

"That's a big leap. The lock is off the gate, so Steve did it?"

"Think about it. We were pretty sure he had a gun. And he was chasing us down. It seemed like he wanted to kill us. He couldn't have ripped the lock off with his bare hands. Yeah, the guy's a hulk. But he's not that strong. I guess he could have used bolt cutters. Do you think he wanted to drown us? Or just scare us away?"

"You're way ahead of me, Detective. But it does

make sense. I was just hoping we were wrong about a gun."

An odd feeling came over me. It was like we were being watched. I crouched, almost expecting bullets to fly. But we had the storm going for us. Our buddies were probably laying low.

For the moment, the weather actually helped us. But we had to keep moving. Soon we'd be even wetter and colder. I glanced over at Juan. A shiver rippled across his shoulders. His teeth began to chatter.

"My hands and feet are numb," he said. "I can't seem to warm up."

"Let's get off the dam. Then we'll head back to Cub Lake."

"What's your plan?"

"We'll have to wing it. Who knows what Steve has waiting for us?"

We headed down a trail that led to a ridge. It was the same spot where I'd seen Steve throw a match. That was just a few hours ago. But it felt more like days.

Juan closed his eyes. "I could fall asleep standing here."

This wasn't good. Juan was showing signs of hypothermia.

"We have to keep moving," I said.

"Where are we going?" Juan mumbled.

Add confusion to the list. "To help Maria," I said. "Did you forget?"

"Oh yeah." Juan took a step and tripped.

I tried to catch him. But he fell. His head barely missed a rock.

Chapter 11

Exposed

Juan lay on the ground. He was curled up in a ball. Leaves clung to his hair. His clothes were soaked.

I crouched next to him. "Are you okay?" I knew he wasn't. But I wanted him to talk.

"I think so, Abuela."

Juan was losing it. He'd just called me "Grandmother." Somehow I had to get him warm. "Take that shirt off." I tossed him a towel. "Dry yourself with this. Then you can put on my jacket." We had now run out of clothes.

Juan stared up at me. He had a dazed look on his face. After a few seconds, he got to his feet. It took him forever to get the shirt off. But finally he put on the jacket.

"Eat this," I said. I gave him a piece of beef jerky. I doubted it would help. But it couldn't hurt. It's what any decent grandma would do. "Come on. Let's go. While there's still light."

Juan followed me like a puppy. I already missed his wisecracks. Now I had to look after him and find Maria too.

What if I got hypothermia? It was possible. My clothes were soaked. I'd be better off naked. Bears walked around that way. Why not me? The thought nearly made me laugh. Juan wasn't the only one who was losing it.

Hiding out suddenly sounded good. Let them all deal with their own problems. It made me question my ancestry. The Cloud people were not cowards.

A little bit of DNA was all we had in common. Right now, I was not feeling brave. But in their spirit, I worked up my courage. If they could battle Incas, I could face Steve.

We came to a path. It cut through the woods. I hoped it led to the main road. If not, we'd be seeing Steve. And then he would kill us. Or maybe he'd be nice. We'd sing songs around the campfire. I laughed out loud. Hysteria was a few giggles away.

Juan laughed too. But it wasn't normal. This laugh was a high-pitched cackle. His face looked just as odd. It was ghostly white. There was no emotion in his eyes. His cheeks were sunken.

I wanted to hurry. But the brush slowed us down. I

used my end of the paddle to cut through it. Just ahead I saw a dim light. It came from inside a tent. This was Steve's campsite. The soft glow was almost welcoming.

A twig snapped under my shoe. I froze. Juan ran into me from behind.

Chapter 12

Stressed

I held my breath. Any second Steve would come running. But nothing happened. The only noise was Juan's breathing in my ear.

I crept forward. Juan followed me. We were a few feet from the tent. That's when I crouched behind a boulder. I signaled for Juan to get down.

A figure danced inside the tent. It swayed and stopped. Shouts and laughter floated out.

Juan mumbled something. I put my finger over my lips. "Shhh."

"Leave her alone!" Chris yelled.

Chris defending Maria? That was a surprise.

"Yeah, let her go," Tyler said. It was less an order than a whine.

"Don't forget who has the gun," Steve said.

My stomach lurched. I was right. There was a gun.

"Let's get this show going," Steve said. "You said your dad has cash. How much?"

After a minute of silence, there was a bright flash of lightning. Rain pelted the ground.

I moved closer to the tent. Juan followed.

"Answer me," Steve said.

One of the canvas walls bulged. A body pressed into it.

"I don't know," Tyler finally said.

"What about jewelry?"

Tyler spoke again. His voice was even weaker. I couldn't make out his words.

"Relax, Tyler," Chris said. "You look like you're about to puke. There's nothing to worry about. I'm not going to break into your house. Your parents don't have anything I want."

"No one's breaking in," Steve said. "We have permission. Right, Tyler?"

Tyler let out another squeak.

"When did you say your parents were leaving?" Steve asked.

"I thought we were buying Tyler's gun," Chris said. "For target shooting. You didn't say anything about—"

"I changed my mind," Steve said.

There seemed to be a scuffle inside the tent. It looked like it might fall.

"I thought Mary could give us a dance. I bet she's got the moves," Steve said. "Right, Tyler?"

My heart was beating fast. Juan slouched against me. His breathing was heavy.

"A quickie," Steve said. "Then we'll head over to Tyler's place. How does that sound, boys?"

"Leave her alone," Chris said.

"Get that gun out of my face!" Maria yelled. "I'm leaving."

Every muscle in my body clenched. My first thought was to rush the tent. But I held myself back. I wasn't crazy yet. Going up against Steve could get me killed. My next move would have to be well timed.

Chapter 13

Warrior

For now Maria was okay. It was good to hear the fight in her voice. This was the girl I knew. She didn't follow the crowd. If kids did the wrong thing, she'd speak up. When Juan was bullied, Maria stood up for him. It was the right thing to do.

I glanced at Juan. Now he was lying down. His part of the paddle was cradled in his arms.

Voices still came from the tent. But now they were muffled. I strained to listen over my pounding heart. Then Steve's laughter rang out. It sounded like thunder.

"Where do you think you're going? It's a long walk to town," Steve said.

"Leave me alone," Maria said. The fight had left her voice. Now it trembled.

The tent rocked and nearly toppled over. I jumped up.

Juan sat up and leaned on his elbow. "What's going on?"

"Quiet," I whispered. It was good to hear him speak. "Wait here."

I dropped my bag. Carrying my paddle, I crept toward the tent.

"Let's have some fun," Steve said.

Suddenly I slipped. I'd fallen forward into a puddle. Mud covered my hands and legs. I bit back a cry of pain. This was a fight I was ready for. I gripped the paddle like a bat.

"Get back, Chris!" Steve said.

The crack of a gunshot rang out. A bullet ripped through the tent. Maria screamed. Then there was silence. Nothing moved. Even the wind had stopped.

"I warned you," Steve said after a minute.

Bodies pressed into the tent. By now I knew Steve's shadow. This was my chance. I aimed the paddle at his back and swung. He landed with a thud. Stakes ripped from the ground. Part of the tent fell.

Steve moved. He began to groan. Without thinking, I hit his head. The contact with his skull made a crunching noise. I stepped back, stunned by my strength. Maybe I *was* a warrior.

"What's going on?" Chris yelled.

The rest of the tent fell. Bodies came crawling out. Maria and Chris were first. Tyler was next.

Chapter 14

Humble

Maria stumbled over to me. "Raul?" She patted my arm. "I knew you'd come back."

"I thought the river would stop you," Chris said.

"Why'd you do it?" I shook my head. "We almost drowned."

Chris lifted his hands in a half surrender. "Hey, it wasn't my idea. Steve planned the whole thing. I found out after he shot the lock off the gate. Anyway, I'm glad you're okay."

I looked at Maria. For a second, I thought about putting my arms around her. But I wouldn't want to let go. Then I'd really embarrass myself. Instead, I gave her a smile and stepped away.

"Where's the gun?" I asked Chris.

"Right here," he said.

The gun was so black, it blended in with the shadows. Chris held it upside down by the trigger. It dangled between his fingers.

Dark circles framed Chris's eyes. Maria and Tyler looked just as bad. I'm sure I did too. We were all tired and dazed. A moan coming from the tent reminded us. Steve was still inside.

"What are we going to do with him?" Maria asked.

"Tie him up," Tyler said.

"There's rope in my bag," I said.

Tyler held out his hand to Chris. "Now give me my gun."

"Hold on now," Chris said. "You're the one who wanted to sell it." Chris shoved the gun at Tyler. "Because Daddy wouldn't pay for a new car."

Tyler backed away. "Be careful with that. You can hold on to it for now."

Maria jabbed Tyler in the chest. "You said this was going to be fun. We'd hang out at your friend's campsite. Roast some marshmallows. Well, look at us now. I'm done with—"

"Enough arguing," I said. "Juan needs our help."

"*Dónde está* Juan?"

I hadn't heard Maria speak Spanish in years.

"Over there somewhere." I pointed at the boulders along the edge of the campsite. "He's waiting for me."

"Is he okay?" she asked.

I shook my head. "I think it's hypothermia."

"Oh no!" Maria motioned from Steve to Chris to Tyler. "None of this was my idea."

I shrugged. Maria wouldn't hurt anyone. But I didn't know about Mary. And lately, it was Mary making the choices.

The people she hung out with weren't great. That didn't change the way I felt about her.

"Explain later," I said. "I need to get Juan." I hoped he hadn't wandered off or passed out.

Unbalanced

Tyler looked nervous. He bounced on the tips of his toes. It seemed he would blast off at any moment. "Let's get out of here." He ran off toward the parking lot. His only concern was himself.

"Hang on," I said. "I've got to find Juan."

"I'll help." Chris and Maria had said it at the same time.

Maria looked down the trail toward Tyler. He'd stopped and was checking his pockets. "Forget something?" she called. "You're going to need your keys."

"Crap," Tyler said. He ran back to the campsite.

"Steve has them," Maria said. "Remember?"

Tyler and Maria walked over to the tent. They lifted a corner of the canvas. Steve lay there. He was still out if it.

"Think he'll wake up?" Tyler asked.

"I'll do it." Maria reached into Steve's pants pocket. She pulled out two sets of keys. "We'll take his keys too. That'll slow him down."

Tyler took off down the trail again. After a few steps, he glanced back. "Are you guys coming or what?"

Maria and I ignored him.

"Is there a phone signal here?" I asked.

"No," Maria said. "But it doesn't matter. Steve took our phones. He threw them into the lake. Are we going to take Juan to the hospital? We can call the police from there."

"We have to find him first," I said.

Tyler was back. "What are you saying about police?" he asked. "No one is calling the cops."

"Listen to your boyfriend, Mary." It was Chris. He turned the gun on us. What happened to nice Chris?

Tyler stepped toward Maria. "Yeah. Listen to me," he said.

Maria glared at Chris and Tyler. "You both screwed up," she said. "First, you hang out with a creep like Steve. Then you, Tyler, demand more money for the gun. That's what set him off."

I could have added my own observation. Maria's judgment was pretty bad too. She should have stuck with me and Juan. None of this would have happened. Instead, I focused on Chris and the gun. His hand was shaking. I was pretty sure he wouldn't shoot us on purpose. But the gun could go off by accident.

"Come on, Chris," I said. "Quit messing around. Juan needs us. We have to go before Steve wakes up."

Steve was now curled up in a ball. The position made him look small and weak.

Chris aimed the gun at Maria. "Not until she agrees. No police."

"Yeah," Tyler said. "No police." He stepped toward us and raised his fist.

"What are you going to do? Hit me?" Maria said. Her eyes shifted between Tyler and Chris. "Both of you back off. I've had enough of the bullying."

I stepped in front of Maria. "Everyone calm down."

Chris tightened his grip on the gun. His eyes narrowed. I guessed this was his tough look. But his shaking hand gave him away. All I saw was the goofy kid who used to make us laugh.

He wasn't a stoner or a gangster or whatever this character was. Chris was my childhood friend. Like Maria, I would always care about him.

Just then I heard the rustle of leaves. Crickets chirped. There was the long hoot of an owl. Two shorter hoots followed that. The noises drew my attention. These were from nature. This is why people came to the woods. It was a peaceful place. Until today.

I thought of my parents. Had they begun to worry yet? They probably had no idea I was in trouble. Why would they? I was out doing my favorite sport.

A loud crash broke the silence. Branches snapped. Leaves crunched. This wasn't from nature. Someone or something was running. Then a figure came out from the shadows.

Chapter 16

Mad

Juan staggered like a drugged animal. His end of the paddle was propped on one shoulder. Maria covered her mouth with her hand. I shot her a look. It said, *No! Don't let on!* Then Juan stopped. He stood hunched over, looking grim.

Chris still held the gun on us. Somehow he hadn't heard all the noise. Who knew what he might do if he turned around. I had to get the gun.

My eyes darted from Chris to Juan and back again. This was my only chance. "Bear! Run!" I shouted.

"It's a grizzly!" Maria yelled.

Chris sprang forward. He stumbled and lowered the gun. I held my breath, hoping he would drop it. Juan headed back toward the woods.

"Hey, Juan," Tyler said. "We were coming to get you."

He chose this moment to open his big mouth. I'd always thought he was clueless. This proved I was right.

Chris spun around. The gun swung with him. Juan lurched forward. Water still squished in his shoes. His hair clung to his scalp. He made a soft growling sound.

"Don't move," Chris said. His hand shook as he aimed at Juan.

Juan stumbled forward. I doubted he even understood what Chris was saying.

Chris steadied his aim. "Don't come any closer. I'll shoot if you do."

Something in me snapped. Whether it was worry and exhaustion or pure frustration, I wasn't sure. The feelings boiled up inside me. I reached for the gun. Chris ducked.

"What are you thinking?" I said. I took a step toward Chris. "Are you really going to shoot Juan? Maria? All of us?"

"Maybe." Chris's shoulders drooped. "I don't know."

Juan plodded over to us. Maria grabbed him by the neck of his shirt. Then she looked at Chris.

"You tried to protect me," she said. "Without you, we wouldn't have gotten away from Steve. I'll tell the police all of that. I'll stand up for you."

I nodded. "We both will."

"Me too," Juan slurred.

There was no way he knew what we were talking about.

"It won't matter," Chris said. "I'm going to jail."

"Remember when we were kids?" I said. "We were there for each other."

Chris raised the gun.

What did I say? I thought we were making progress.

"Oh yeah?" Chris said. "What about the last few years. Where have you been?"

Chapter 17

Clouded Thinking

You're right, Chris. I wish we'd stuck together. Those were good times. But we're here now." I looked at Maria and Juan. "Let us help you."

"Please," Maria said.

Darkness had settled over the campsite. The night air was freezing. I wasn't just frozen cold. It felt like I was stuck in time.

Maria helped me make a fire. Maybe Juan would warm up.

The flames made me sleepy. I thought about the river. Juan and I had nearly been killed. Now I imagined being back in the water. Floating calmly with the current. Slowly slipping under the surface. Feeling a sense of peace.

A noise stirred me from my dream. It was the chatter of Juan's teeth. If he didn't warm up soon, he'd pass out.

What was worse? Dying from cold or being shot by Steve? It was all the same. Drowning would have been easier.

Chris rubbed his chin with the gun. "I'm done," he said.

I took a deep breath. What had he meant by that?

"Life is too hard," he said.

Maria, Tyler, and I stepped toward him.

"I'm just so tired of it all." Chris pressed the gun to his head.

"No!" we all cried out.

This couldn't be real. I wanted to hide like a child. Maybe it would all go away. Instead, I kept my eyes on Chris. When he looked at me, I held his gaze. Without words, I tried to connect with him. Maybe he'd read my eyes. *Set the gun down*. But I couldn't see past the sadness.

Chris pushed the gun into his temple. My mind raced. What could I say? No words could change the misery he felt. Nothing would undo his mom's leaving. His friends had all gone separate ways. He was left to deal with life by himself.

The Chris I knew as a kid was still there. I just had to reach him. "Look at me, Chris. You don't want to do this. Remember when we were kids? You were the one we all looked up to. In our eyes, no one could do anything better. No one had a better sense of humor. That Chris was full of life. He had a bright future. *You* have a bright future."

We stared at each other. His eyes were big dark pools. It made me think of a bottomless pit. Had I lost him forever? Had we all fallen into some kind of black hole?

Chris dropped the gun. It bounced and fired off a shot. Chaos followed. Tyler hit the ground. Maria screamed. I jumped and Juan swayed. He looked like he might collapse.

Chris sat down on a boulder. He tucked his hands beneath his thighs. "This is messed up," he said.

Just then Tyler jumped up. Our eyes met for a second. Then we both went for the gun. Tyler shoved me. But I got to it first.

Guarded

I scooped up the gun and held it behind my back. Tyler stood in front of me. He shoved my chest. "Hand it over," he said.

"No way."

Juan walked up to us. The paddle was raised over his head. It looked like he was about to strike Tyler.

"Put it down," I said to Juan.

He lowered the paddle but kept circling us.

Maria stepped between Tyler and me. She motioned with her hand. "Give me the gun."

I didn't move.

"You can trust me," she said. Her eyes narrowed. "Besides, it's safer with me."

Now I held the gun by its barrel with two fingers. "What do you mean by that?"

"The way you're handling it. You don't know what you're doing."

"And you do?" I asked. "Since when?"

"My dad takes me target shooting. When did you stop trusting me?"

We stared at each other for a long time. She finally nodded, as if responding to a question. Were we thinking the same thing? I doubted it. Maria hadn't been aware of my feelings for years. Still, this could be a beginning. Maybe we could get back to being friends.

I handed her the gun. She ejected the bullets and shoved them into her pocket.

Juan came up to me. "Are you okay, Abuela?"

"Abuela?" Tyler said. He started to laugh.

"It's not funny," Maria said. "Juan isn't well." Then tears rolled down her cheeks.

I gave her an awkward pat. She drew in a deep breath and wiped her face. Then I turned to Juan. "Leave Tyler alone."

Juan's shoulders slouched. His whole body shivered. He could barely hold himself up. Maria helped him walk back to the fire.

Chris cleared his throat. "Look, I'm sorry. I never would have shot you guys. I don't know what I was doing."

Maria's eyes met mine. We had to be wondering the same thing. Would Chris have shot himself?

Chris opened his mouth to speak.

I raised my hand. "We can talk on the way to the hospital. And there's plenty of time after that too."

"He's right," Maria said. "Together, we can get back to normal."

She'd made it sound so easy. We'd find those magic words. They would make everything better. Chris would be okay. At least he'd be the fun-loving kid we used to know. We had to try. That kid still existed.

Chris dropped his head. He gave a slight nod.

Chapter 19

Strain

Maria looked at me. "Let's tie up Steve. Then we can get out of here. Where's your rope?"

I walked over to my bag. That's when I heard angry voices. It was Maria and Tyler. They were arguing. But I couldn't tell what it was about.

Juan circled Tyler. Once in a while, he'd poke Tyler with the paddle. It would have been funny except for the seriousness of Juan's condition. At least it kept him moving.

By now Chris had come over to help me. We stood over Steve.

"I wish I could start today over. None of this would have happened," Chris said. "If I could, I'd go back and redo the past few years."

"I know," I said. "I'd do a lot of things differently too.

But things can be different starting now." I handed him a piece of rope. "Here. You tie Steve's legs."

As I tied Steve's arms, I saw burn marks. I looked over at Chris, who had also seen them. His eyes were wide. We didn't speak.

Chris headed back to the group. "Are you coming?" he called to me.

"In a minute." I studied the scars, trying to read them like they were clouds. But they only brought up more questions. Who or what caused the scars and why? Had Steve been abused? Is that why he turned violent?

I put the tent canvas around him. He'd stay warm until the cops got there. In a way, I felt sorry for him. His scars were deep. They weren't only physical. They were mental. Did anyone in his life care about him? Now I doubted it.

Just then I heard Tyler's voice. "Get away from me, Stinky Feet."

What was Juan up to now? I spun around. He was swinging the paddle over his head. With each swing, Tyler ducked. He was nearly struck a few times.

"Stop!" I called out. I took the paddle from Juan and dropped it.

Maria stood facing Tyler. Her hands were on her hips. "We're going to the police. That's final."

Tyler grabbed Maria by the arm. "Who put you in charge?" he said. She yanked her arm away from him.

"Hey, Tyler," I said. "Maybe you should stay here with your buddy Steve."

"No more talking." Maria shoved the gun into the waistband of her shorts. "I'm out of here." She headed down the trail.

"Hold on," Tyler said. "You're not going anywhere."

He took off running. Chris and I followed closely behind. Just before we could reach him, he grabbed Maria. He had her by the hair. She bent forward, trying to twist from his grip. But he pulled harder. Her head flew backward.

Chris hooked his arm around Tyler's neck. "Let go of her," Chris said. He tightened his hold. "Do it or die!"

Tyler loosened his grip on Maria. She rubbed her head. "I'm going to the car," she said. I saw her push the gun farther down in her waistband.

"Do you have any rope left?" Chris asked.

"Yeah. I'll go get it." After a minute, I was back. Chris held Tyler while I tied his wrists.

"Hey. You're hurting me," Tyler said. His wrists strained against the rope.

Chapter 20

Weathered

Juan," I called. "Come on."

Juan came up the trail. He was about to hit Tyler.

"It's okay," I said. "We've got him."

Juan lowered his fists. His eyes looked empty. There was no emotion, only exhaustion. All he could do was yawn. I knew how he felt.

Chris led Tyler down the trail. By now Maria was out of sight.

Juan and I walked side by side. The moon lit our way. Once in a while, he'd stray off the path. I'd gently pull him back.

When we got to the parking lot, I saw Tyler's SUV. A rusted-out truck sat beside it. I guessed it was Steve's.

Tyler was a piece of work. He stole his dad's gun to

get back at him. For what? For not buying his spoiled son a new car? It was insane. Pathetic was more like it.

Maria stood next to the SUV. She held a blanket out to me. "Juan should get out of those clothes."

I turned to tell Juan. But he'd already stripped down to his underwear.

"Way more than I want to see," Maria said.

I laughed. "Tell me about it." I put the blanket around Juan.

"I'll drive," Maria said. She reached into Tyler's pocket and pulled out his keys.

"Crank the heat," I said.

"Untie me," Tyler said. "I won't try anything."

Maria shook her head. She climbed in behind the steering wheel and started the engine.

Chris held Tyler by the arm. "You're in back, Tyler. Juan, you get in front."

Chris and I sat on either side of Tyler. The car was now warm. Juan's head was back against the seat. His eyes closed.

We rode along the bumpy road. Maria headed for the highway. I called the cops to report Steve. They said they'd be out to get him.

We'd have to get Juan's truck another time. For now, I just wanted to get back to the city. I wanted Juan to be okay.

Chris stared out the window. "Remember in the fourth grade? You talked about being a Cloud warrior?"

"Yeah. You laughed at me. All the kids did."

"That was just a cover. I was going along with the crowd. But I thought you were cool."

I saw Maria's eyes in the rearview mirror. She was looking at me. "Read the sky, Raul."

I looked out the window. Thin clouds streaked across the moon. Stars filled the sky. My abilities were limited to clouds. And I needed daylight to read them. Even then I could only predict. Would it be good weather or bad?

The stars held different secrets. They spoke of places beyond my imagination.

"The stars are a mystery. Kind of like you, Maria. I can only read clouds. At least I thought I could."

Maria still believed in me. I wanted to live up to that. Be her hero. But today I'd failed in many ways. I ignored signs of a storm. I'd failed to read the river. And I felt like I let Juan down.

Our eyes met again in the mirror. "There is no doubt in my mind," Maria said. "You're a Cloud warrior."

The rest of the ride was silent. All I could foresee now was a long night. There would be questions from the cops. We'd be with Juan in the ER for hours. And we'd have to explain it all to our parents.

This day had been a disaster. Everything that could go wrong did go wrong. It had been a perfect storm. But in the end, more went right. I'd faced nature and my past. My friends and I had come full circle. I knew who they were now. And they were going to be okay.

WANT TO KEEP READING?

9781680214789

Turn the page for a sneak peek
at another book in the Monarch
Jungle series.

Give Me a Break

Being a responsible teenager has its pluses. Your parents trust you. They do things like buy you a car. Any teen would be happy about that. What you don't know is how long they've waited for this moment. Now you can drive your little sister places. That's what happened to me.

Today is Saturday. It's noon. But I'm still in my pj's. I settle in for a long session of texting. My best friend, Liv, broke up with her boyfriend. I've heard it all before. They've broken up three times.

She just sent me a long message. It's mostly about how mean Mark is. He controls everything Liv does. It makes me sad for her. I hope she leaves him for good this time.

I start to text when there's a knock on my door. I'm sure it's my sister, Teera.

"Go away! I'm busy!"

"Tansy?"

Oops. It's Mom.

"Can I come in?"

"Sure," I call out.

The door opens. Teera is there too. I know what this means. She wants to go somewhere.

"Your sister needs to go to the library."

I don't want to do it. But those were the terms when I got the car.

"Fine," I say.

"Don't be too long," Mom says. "We're having barbecue. Dad's making ribs."

Yum. I'm already hungry. Mom leaves the room. Teera stays behind.

"Will you help me with my book report?"

"What's it about?"

Teera looks at her notebook. "Wyatt Earp and the Cowboys," she reads.

"From the Old West? I saw a movie once. Wyatt Earp was a sheriff. And there was a gang of outlaws. They were called the Cowboys. That's all I know."

"Then just give me one of your old reports. I can copy it."

"That's cheating. Besides, they're all on the Middle Ages. And sorcery. It's too scary for you."

"Ooh. You mean witches? Cool."

"You're not using my reports. Now get out, please. I need to get dressed."

My phone is going off again. I didn't answer Liv's text yet. And now she thinks I'm ignoring her.

"I'll meet you in the car!" I tell Teera.